STATES OF BEING

By Susan F. Banks

Red Souls of the Underworld Series
Red Souls
Wall of Unknowing
Wheel of Augustus

'Soul never dies. Everything else is temporary.'
---- Gem, the Guardian of the Gate

INTRODUCTION

States of Being introduces you the series **Red Souls of the Underworld** by Susan F Banks.

As a unique creation in the fantasy genre, the series combines fantasy, science and supernatural suspense in a story of friendship, love and danger. It is a lucid dream in written form.

What follows are excerpts and outtakes from the series.

For more information, visit **susanfbanks.com** where you will find a song list that accompanies each book of the series, along with interviews and blog posts.

Prologue

The Astral Gate separates the Physical and Astral planes. It is protected by an enclave of Guardians assigned to every major city of the world. In Los Angeles, the Guardian of the Gate is a 170-year-old Astral Master named Gem, of Jamaican descent and born in the pre-Civil War South. She has maintained the Gate and protected L.A. from Jat the Deceiver, Lord of the Underworld for over 120 years.

Gem is a strong Master, but a young one, and practitioner of the Freezing Breath. She needs the help of a Circle of dedicated people to help her defend the Gate – a Listener who can hear astral voices, a Ring Thrower who can focus the energy of the Circle, and Warriors of Heart and Steel who will defend them at all costs. Gem found such people, but they were young, self-absorbed, and oblivious to the dangers facing their city. Gem opened their eyes and expanded their awareness of the awful plans Jat has for L.A. Thus, the Circle of Augustus rose again in the modern age.

Jat planted a virulent and invasive crystal underneath Los Angeles, and Red Souls used it as a highway between the Astral and Physical worlds. they could bypass the Gate and travel undetected by the Guardian. Swarming over the city in swirls of glittering red smoke, they attacked the minds of humans and drove the most vulnerable to rage and despair. Chaos broke out in the streets. It was just the beginning.

Main Characters

Gem – Guardian of the Astral Gate

Circle of Augustus:
Willet Du Place
Audrey Du Place
Dean Simmons
Thomas Jefferson (TJ) Barlow

Jat the Deceiver – Lord of the Underworld

Jat the Deceiver

The creator of illusions and ruler of demons is known by
many names - Jat the Deceiver, Lord of the Underworld,
Creator of Nightmares and Master of Despair. It was Jat who
seeded the earth underneath Los Angeles with the insidious
crystal that wreaked havoc and destruction in the city.
Swarms of Red Souls escaped from the crystal in clouds of red
smoke no one could see, to infect people with thoughts of
anger, lust and greed. People became confused. They forgot
the most basic facts about their lives, stumbled through the
streets and hid in their houses. Jat would take advantage of
the city's weakened condition. He wants it for his own.

Out of shadow, doubt grows; hope dies; without hope, despair chills the soul. Jat seeks to control people, not through conquest, but through deception. His illusions trick the mind and enflame emotions. When people accept the thoughts planted by the Red Souls, they turn on each other in anger and discontent. Jat takes over such a weak and broken place and rules it as he pleases. Now L.A. teeters on the brink of an even darker future. Unless there is someone to stop it.

The Guardian of the Astral Gate

From a high vantage point at Griffith Park, Gem scanned the skies over Los Angeles, searching for a breach of the Astral Gate. As Guardian of said Gate, it was her responsibility to protect L.A., from ocean to desert, against attacks from the Astral Underworld. So it had been for one hundred and twenty years. Lately, the attacks were coming harder and faster. She felt an ache in her chest whenever a breach occurred, and her chest was getting sore.

Northeast of downtown, she spotted a phantom hole hovering above the city. Red, glittering smoke rained on the streets below. "There it is, Dora," she said to the big black Labrador retriever sitting at her feet. "The third breach this week. Above Covina, I would say. They certainly do make an entrance."

Dora blinked her golden eyes, and the white patch on her forehead furrowed. Dora's physical size and presence intimidated, as one would expect of the Hound of Hell. No one who heard her thunderous growl or saw her three-inch canines extend out of slobbering jaws would dare threaten the Guardian when Dora was by her side.

Guardian and Hound headed for the Jeep parked nearby. The gritty static of a shortwave radio mounted on the dashboard came from the police band. It spat out reports of a fight among neighbors at an apartment complex in West Covina. The situation had all the earmarks of a Red Souls attack – sudden fighting, weapons drawn, and young children in harm's way. Someone had a knife to the apartment manager's throat, all for no apparent reason in a usually quiet neighborhood.

Gem headed down the freeway as traffic conveniently split in front of her. With her foot heavy on the gas, the Jeep practically flew. She reached the neighborhood in West Covina and slowed the Jeep to a roll. As she expected, red smoke churned and glittered in the air over the apartment.

Red Souls break out of the Astral Underworld and travel in smoke in the physical world. They come to prey on the passions of human beings by planting vivid suggestions in their consciousness. Anger, violence, lust, greed - whatever weakness a person had, no matter how deeply buried, the Souls would exploit it. Every time a person accepted the suggestions as his own desires and acted on them, Red Souls enjoyed the vicarious thrill, and the Gate became progressively weaker.

Gem parked down the street from the apartments. "The attack is underway, my dear," she said. "I hope we are not too late." Dora lolled her long pink tongue and whined softly.

Gem closed her eyes, took deep, steady breaths, and chanted under her breath, tuning herself to the astral rate of vibration like a tuning fork. *HU. Na-u-ma-um-na. HU.* Decades of practice helped her ignore the din of the city and listen for the familiar soft buzz in her left ear. Thoughts drifted through her mind, nagging for attention. She released them one by one and focused on the inner screen between her eyes. She waited for the pinpoint of white light to pierce the darkness. Suddenly there it was, so small, but rushing toward her, growing larger.

Light crashed over her. A cool wave rolled into the top of her head, down her spine and tingled in the soles of her feet. Ocean surf whispered, mingling with the rise and fall of her breath. Her astral consciousness peeled away from her physical body and moved through the door of the Jeep enveloped in luminous pink light. Dora emerged in her own astral form, tail wagging happily. They moved in an undetectable blur of speed to the apartment building.

A bank of hedges hid the pool area in back of the apartment from street view but could not hide the angry voices. Gem floated through the hedges to the pool on a wave of astral energy with Dora bobbing along at her side. People in swimming suits and beachwear stood on each side of a pool, yelling and waving their arms at each other. Children huddled underneath pool chairs covering themselves with towels. The silver of weapons flashed in some hands.

At the head of the pool, a man pleaded for help and tried to wriggle away from a larger man choking him with one arm while he waved a knife in his other hand.

The astral bodies of people lost to their own negative emotions look like black and white X-rays. The skeletal figures around the pool hissed at Gem and Dora, crouched low, and covered their skulls with boney arms. Red Souls darted in all directions in streams of smoke. Dora howled, driving away any Soul that dared get too close to Gem.

This was astral L.A., the emotional city, so close to the physical as to appear almost identical but vibrating at a different rate. The hole in the Gate hovered ten feet above the pool, visible only to astral sight. People around the pool were too busy shouting to notice anything. Sparkling red smoke slipped into their noses and mouths. The more they yelled, the more they inhaled it. The glitter in the smoke sparked faster and brighter, excited by all the anger.

The children huddled under chairs glowed pink, and each one twinkled like a star. They could see Gem through their innocent eyes. Their astral bodies slipped out from under the chairs and floated toward her with arms open wide, seeking safety behind her. Dora rumbled a growl of warning at any skeleton who tried to grab a star as it floated past.

"Easy, girl," murmured Gem. "We do not want to scare the little ones."

Gem threw her head back, formed ice and sleet in her mouth and blew out an exuberant spray, showering the skeletons with freezing rain. Her breath sizzled as it hit them. The skeletons wailed and cringed. Their boney appearance faded, and their bodies turned a faint pink. It left them blinking and confused, as if they had awakened from a bad dream. Such was the power of the Guardian's Freezing Breath. It froze negative emotions.

The situation at the head of the pool was trickier. Ruby beads of blood oozed from the manager's throat as the large man pressed the knife against the manager's skin and locked eyes with Gem. Those eyes were black with rage, out of control, caught in the downward pull of negativity. Red Souls encouraged him with their screams. He let the knife slice fully into the flesh of the manager's neck. Gem blew a freezing breath at the two men, but the man with the knife would not let go.

The front of the manager's shirt was now drenched with his own blood. She had to put the knife man in a hard freeze. She seldom used that kind of freeze on anyone. It left a person traumatized, but it could not be helped. The knife man held on to his anger too stubbornly. Gem had to act before the manager bled out completely.

She pursed her lips, formed an arrow-headed projectile of ice on her tongue, and spit it at the knife man with the force of a bullet. It hit him between the eyes. His eyes glazed over, and his aura turned grey. Frozen solid emotionally, he tilted to the side and fell. The manager collapsed on top of him. They would live, but there was one more problem to solve.

The breach above the pool still festered like a swollen blister. Red smoke oozed through cracks at the edges. Gem gathered another Freezing Breath and exhaled it, icy and strong as a gale. It sent the Red Souls scattering in all directions. They screamed, trying to resist the force of it, regrouped and charged at her. Dora jumped in front of the Guardian, howling with a keening ferocity that made every astral body at the pool cover their ears. The smoke swirled away from Dora's howl as if it was a sonic shield. Another blast from Gem sent most of the smoke rolling up through the hole in the sky and out of sight.

Gem layered sheets of ice on the inflamed surface of the breach. It healed as it cooled and became nothing more than a shimmer above the pool, like sunlight gilding the water. She knew some Red Souls had escaped. They would reappear in the city eventually.

She closed her eyes and listened to the calm roll of ocean waves that signified the astral plane, breathing in synchrony with the waves. In the absolute silence between flow and ebb, she recharged her energy. Dora's wet nose nudging her neck brought her back to physical consciousness. They were sitting in the Jeep.

"Let's take a walk," Gem said. She clicked a leash around Dora's neck.

Gem and Dora walked around to the front of the apartment. Two squad cars and an ambulance parked at the curb, and neighbors gathered on the sidewalk to get a look at someone on a stretcher. The apartment manager lay on it white as a sheet. His astral body hovered above the stretcher, deciding whether to remain or leave the physical body behind.

Two policemen walked out of the complex with the knife man in handcuffs between them. They held him up under his armpits, because he couldn't stand on his own. His body had an ice-blue shimmer about it.

"He is still a bit wobbly," Gem murmured to Dora. "I had to hit him especially hard."

As Gem and Dora returned to the Jeep, the ground shuddered under their feet. Earth tremors were common in LA, but she never took them lightly. In the Jeep, Gem glanced in the mirror. Her chocolate skin glowed with physical and astral energy. Her tight, blonde-tinged brown curls remained in place, but her lipstick had faded. She pulled a tube of Ruby Rosa out of the glove compartment and applied a light coat. The mirror rattled as another tremor rolled beneath the tires.

No time for a hot shower to settle her back into her physical body. The police band squawked about a street fight near Bell Gardens. Once again, tempers had flared, and people threatened each other with weapons. Coincidence? The Guardian did not believe in coincidences. She had to check on it.

Red Souls had found other targets. *That's where they went*, she thought. Those Souls would not escape her again.

The Listener

Willet du Place settled into the soft leather seat of the sedan, tilting it back just a bit, and plugged in her iPod. Chopin's Ballade #1 in G Minor rolled through the surround speakers, pensive and dreamy. She had practiced the piece many times.

She stared through the windshield at the grey streets, exiled to the curb like an unwanted stepchild. Despite the sound-proof sedan, she could hear the crash of cymbals, the thump of the bass drum. Oh, to be normal enough just to walk in, listen to the band, and dance around with Audrey like a crazy teenager.

She turned up the CD, trying to drown out external sounds, and let Chopin's glorious music beguile her into a reverie, and then a dream.

Chopin sat at his piano in a black frock coat, fingers moving over the keys. His back and shoulders swayed with barely contained emotion. Warm, golden waves of music floated through her head. Passionate chords built to thrilling arpeggios. She sighed with contentment.

Chopin stopped. He turned to her with large brown eyes full of sadness. He placed an index finger against his lips.

"Red Souls come," he whispered, and pointed to the street.

Her gaze shifted there, and an overwhelming feeling of déjà vu swept over her. It was him. The guy in the dirty white hoodie and jeans stood on the sidewalk across the street, staring at her. He crept toward the sedan like a cat, one careful foot at a time, looking right and left as he came.

She huddled low and started to tremble. Wailing voices came out of nowhere. She pressed the headphones to her ears to block them out, but the voices surged. 'Burn', they said. 'Burn.' The echo bounced back and forth between her ears, and a headache exploded like fireworks behind her eyes. The man stared at the car for a long moment, their eyes met through the window. He reached out a hand toward the car, and then he burst into flame.

The fire started at his feet and quickly devoured his torso and arms. A cloud of red smoke billowed around him. Flames licked his neck and head, a wild scream of pain exploded from his open mouth, but he never took his eyes from her. He came closer with arms stretched out toward her, screaming. He reached for the car door with flaming hands.

Terror grabbed her by the throat and squeezed. She bolted upright in panic and turned to Chopin. He was gone. She looked out her window at the sidewalk. The burning man had disappeared. Not a spark, not an ash, nothing. *I've finally lost my mind.* Her headache reached migraine strength. She pulled out her phone and called Audrey. The phone rang several times and then went to voicemail. She sent a brief, desperate message, fumbled for the door handle and climbed out of the car.

A deafening barrage of noise hit her hard. Sirens blared and alarms wailed. Helicopter propellers flapped somewhere overhead. People shouted over megaphones. She saw nothing on this street. *What is going on?* She ran down the sidewalk in the direction of the club, zigzagging like a drunk, pressing the headphones to her ears as she ran.

A couple walking in the opposite direction turned to watch her erratic flight. At the door of Club TJ, the sound of music pounded against her already throbbing ear drums. The pain spread from her ears to her forehead and into her neck. She hunched over to clutch her lurching stomach.

The guy at the door stared at her headphones and her obvious discomfort.

"Did you see the accident?" he asked.

"Accident? No, I – no," she stammered. "I need to speak to Audrey du Place. Can you make an announcement or something?"

"The band's playing. It's pretty loud in there."

"I need to speak to Audrey. Now, please. She's my sister."

Sweat trickled down her temples. Her body swayed. She was about to faint. The bouncer's eyes went wide with alarm.

"I'll call the boss. Hold on a sec."

He pulled out a phone and made the call.

"Boss, there's a lady here, asking for an Audrey du Place. Can we make an announcement? She seems to be having some major trouble."

The bouncer listened to brief instructions and hung up.

"The boss'll be right out."

"I don't know the boss. I need Audrey." Willet started to hyperventilate.

"Easy, lady! Boss says he'll hook you up with Audrey. Stay cool a minute."

The Circle

It took all of thirty seconds for "the Boss" to appear at the front door of the club.

"Willet. You're Willet, right? I'm TJ Barlow, Dean's friend. What's wrong?"

"I'm about to be sick. I need Audrey."

"Hey now, let me take you to my office. The door's around the corner. It's a little quieter there. Then we'll find Audrey."

Too shaky to make reasonable decisions, she allowed TJ to lead her away to parts unknown.

She found herself in an office behind a thick padded door, a quieter space though the music still vibrated in the walls. The beat of the bass made her temples throb. Her headache banged in time with the drums. TJ led her to a couch in the corner and helped her lay down.

She put a hand over her eyes, and then sat up suddenly, gulping air.

"I'm gonna hurl."

TJ jumped back several steps. "Whoa! Not here. Use the bathroom, please, through that door."

Willet made a dash into the room he pointed to and slammed the door after her. She went directly to the toilet and gave up her lunch. She ran water and flushed, preparing for the next heave. After several iterations, she had nothing left. She patted cold water on her face, gargled away the bad breath and stumbled out the door. She felt drained and felt sweat dripping on her forehead. She could barely lift her feet to walk.

TJ watched her, offering an arm in case she fell over. "Do you want aspirin, water, or something?"

"No, just Audrey," she whispered.

TJ went to the door, threw it open and hurried into the hall. The booming noise hit her like a brick. She went to the door, swung it closed and fell back against it, pressing her hands against her temples. She staggered back to the couch and fell on it. In minutes, Audrey burst into the room with TJ.

"Will, what are you doing in here? This is so bad for you. What is going on?"

"I had that dream again and this time the guy caught fire! His whole body was burning! I didn't know what to do. The noise outside the car just about killed me. My head is exploding."

Audrey reached for the small purse on her shoulder and pulled out a bottle of yellow pills. The 'super pills,' Willet called them. Audrey extracted one and handed it to her sister. Willet sat up, swallowed the pill, and dropped back on the couch in exhaustion.

"It'll take a few minutes for the meds to work," Audrey explained softly. "She'll feel better soon."

TJ paced between his desk and the couch. "She saw the man on fire? We should tell the police, shouldn't we?"

"No, we shouldn't," Audrey said. "Give us a chance to deal with the headache, and then we can get the full story."

"What can I do?" he asked helplessly. "Can I get her something?"

"Water will help, when she comes to," Audrey replied.

TJ charged out the door again.

Audrey put her hand on her sister's forehead. "Will? Tell me what happened?"

Willet's hands covered her eyes, breath slow, waiting for the medicine to work its magic. She desperately wanted to sleep but tried to talk.

"I thought about running my head into a door it hurt so much. I thought I dreamed it, but everything seemed so real."

"Just a dream," Audrey murmured, placing a hand on her sister's forehead.

"But the exact same dream, Auddie," she said breathlessly. "Chopin played the piano, and then the guy walked toward the car. I thought he would finally break in this time, but his feet caught on fire. Flames shot up his legs and covered him. He screamed, I screamed. There were voices. Silver Voice I always hear came from Chopin, I think. He said something about Red Souls," "What does it mean?"

"I don't know, hon. Dreams are funny that way."

"This was so *not* funny."

"Of course," Audrey soothed her. "I didn't mean humorous funny."

"I messed up your evening. I'm sorry."

"Never mind that. The band is on break, so it should be quiet for a while. Rest now, and then we'll leave. Are you okay alone for a minute? I'd like to tell Dean I'm leaving."

"Go ahead."

Audrey gently slid the headphones from Willet's head, and Willet released a long breath. Although the headphones were very light in weight, they still put pressure on her head. She didn't notice it until it was gone.

"The music sounded hot, Will. I wish you could have heard it. Dean and his band are so cool."

Willet smiled a dreamy smile and winked. "Cool and hot, quite a combination."

"Yeah, you're funny. You must be feeling better. I'll be right back."

Audrey slipped out the big office door and pulled it shut behind her.

Willet lay on the couch with eyes closed, letting the meds take her over. The door rattled and opened again. TJ walked in.

"Here's some water," he said, handing her the bottle. "Feeling better I hope?"

She sat up slowly, twisted the cap off the bottle, slugged back a long swallow, and looked at him with heavy-lidded eyes while she slowly licked her lips. His eyebrows shot up.

"Thanks Mr. Barlow," she wheezed after she drained the bottle. "Sorry for the drama. My life is a mess sometimes. Unfortunately, it affects Audrey."

"Please call me TJ. Dean did mention some health issues. Does this happen often?"

"Things are always happening to me. Fortunately, there are good meds."

TJ gave a small smirk. "Anything interesting you could share?"

His eyes were the green of rolling seas, and his smile warmed her. He reminded her of the precious few summer days at the beach she'd had as a child. The tang of salt in the air, the sea breeze and warm sun on her skin, and the way the waves swooshed and dragged on the sand. It had been a long time since she'd been to a beach.

"I don't think these pills would have the same pleasant effect on you that they have on me. They're very specific for my condition. *You* may get a brain bleed."

"Ouch. No thanks then. So, from what I heard, a man is lying on the street near here in a pile of ash."

Willet got up from the couch with a wobble, rolled her head on her neck and stretched out her shoulders. Her eyes narrowed. "Are you trying to be funny?"

"No, certainly not. It's just... what I heard. What's a guy to think?"

Willet peered at him as if trying to figure out what species of hominid he was. She tilted her head and turned her right ear toward him. They were standing close to each other, close enough that she extended her arm and placed her hand on his chest. He looked down at the small hand but didn't move away.

"You should think about the obstruction you have in the blood flow to your heart. It makes a glubbing sound right about there." She patted the spot on his chest lightly. "You should see a cardiologist."

TJ's megawatt smile faded. He frowned and stepped back from her. "That's not funny either."

"I don't joke about health matters, Mr. Barlow," she said with level calm. "See a doctor."

"What the hell, woman? You're nuts!"

The office door opened again. Dean and Audrey rushed in and stopped short when they found Willet and TJ in a standoff.

"What's going on?" Dean asked, looking from TJ to Willet and back.

"She's trying to tell me I have a heart problem. That's ridiculous, and it's none of her damn business anyway!"

"Why did you say that, Will?" Audrey asked.

"One of the vessels leading to his heart is partially blocked. It makes a particular sound I've heard before, and I just wanted to warn him."

Audrey turned slowly to TJ and took a deep breath. "I know this may seem abrupt, even rude, and I apologize, but Willet can hear things like that. You should probably take her at her word."

"She hears things, alright. She's a mental patient. She needs to be sedated," TJ growled.

Dean cleared his throat and stepped between them. "I see everyone is on edge, so Audrey, why don't you take Willet to my house until the gig is over? She can check out the place before construction starts."

TJ snorted with irritation. "I don't need a damn babysitter. You can leave too."

"I have to go back on stage for the second set. Audrey? Willet? Okay to travel?"

Willet turned to TJ. "I do thank you for your help, Mr. Barlow. I just wanted to help you in return."

TJ watched the sisters walk out the door, and then kicked it shut with a bang.

"Those women will ruin your life," TJ said in a low, angry growl. "Rethink the job, my friend. It's not worth it, whatever they're paying."

Dean shook his head. "They have issues, sure, but Willet has amazing hearing, beyond the normal. She heard my truck driving to her house from miles away."

"I don't care. No one can hear what's going on in someone else's body, unless he's a doctor with a stethoscope."

"Still, it wouldn't hurt to check it out," Dean said. "When did you see a doctor last?"

"I'm not seeing a damn doctor, not on her say-so anyway."

"Forget that. Everyone needs a checkup once in a while. You could prove her wrong."

TJ lightened a little at that thought. "Yes. I could, couldn't I? Maybe I'll do that. It would serve her right, the smug little freak."

"Harsh words, dude. She's not that way. Anyway, I gotta get back and start the set."

TJ stood in his office deep in thought after Dean left. He stared at his hands, felt his neck, and put a hand on his chest where Willet had touched him. His heart beat steady under his palm. He grunted in satisfaction.

I'm only twenty-eight, eat well, I work out. I'm totally healthy. There's nothing wrong with me, nothing at all.

The Wall

The Circle piled into the sedan parked in the driveway. It was a cozy fit even in such a roomy car. Gem took the passenger seat with Dora tucked under her feet on the floorboard. Willet and TJ sat in the back seat. Dean drove, and Audrey perched between him and Gem. It could have been mistaken for a happy outing with friends if it were not for their ominous destination.

The Wall was farther away than it appeared from Pine Siskin House. The drive took an hour. Judging from Willet's panicked breathing and her desperate attempts to press the headphones harder to her ears, the static hiss had increased to uncomfortable levels. The sedan lurched forward at over ninety miles per hour. Everyone held their breath.

"Dean, slow down, you're going too fast," Audrey exclaimed, clutching her shoulder belt.

"My foot isn't even on the gas!" Dean said pounding his foot on the brake as the car picked up speed. "It's like a magnet pulling on us. I can't stop it."

"We will hit the Wall with force," Gem said calmly. "Secure your seat belts."

The sedan was almost flying, tires barely touching the ground. The scenery outside blurred and the Wall loomed large ahead. When they hit, it sucked them in. The sedan vaulted off the ground into an atmosphere thick as Jell-O. It spun and somersaulted like a slow-motion bowling ball. Sparks flew off the grille and across the hood. One of the back doors swung open and banged back and forth. TJ reached for it and fell head-first out the door.

Willet screamed. "No, No! Stop the car! Thomas fell out!"

....

TJ Barlow reached for the handle when the sedan door opened, but the door swung beyond his reach. He made a grab for it, lost his balance, and fell out head-first into the Wall of Unknowing, rolling, flailing and cursing his own stupidity all the way down. The thick atmosphere seemed to cushion his fall otherwise he'd drop like a rock. Instead, he tumbled, almost in slow motion, and then fell on his butt with a soft thud. He closed his eyes, lying flat on the ground to assess injuries and regain his wits. *Arms and legs are moving. Tailbone feels bruised.* When he opened his eyes, he couldn't make out where he was or what anything was around him. Narrow bands of fuzzy light streaked left and right like bad reception on an old black and white TV. Visually, everything looked fractured. The hairs stood up on his arms. He rolled to his feet and took a minute to balance. Unsure how close anything was, he held out his arms, walked unsteadily toward one shape and laid hands on it. It felt hard and rough - stucco. He stamped his feet - standing on pavement. *If I can't see, how can*

I get out of here?

"Hello! Hello!" he called out, turning in a circle. "Is anybody there?" It was like shouting in an empty room. He was inside the Wall Gem warned them about, and he was alone. Could it get any worse? Well, he could think of a few ways...

Where were Dean and the rest of the Circle? He got angry with himself. *Should have followed my instincts and gone home.* Now he was lost, and who did he have to thank? It always came back to Gem. *Damn that woman.* He wished she were here right now. After she rescued him, he'd tell her off in no uncertain terms. He squinted and tried to find something identifiable nearby. The blur gave him eye strain when he tried to see through it. He thought of Willet with a twinge of pain. She'd be distraught, and insist they look for him. Could they find him in all this fuzz? The Wall they saw from the house had covered the western border of Riverside County. That was a big area to search.

He shuffled forward with both arms extended in front of him, trying not to bump into anything. After several steps, he felt the edge of a curb beneath his left foot just before his ankle collapsed. He fell, landing hard on his right elbow and hip. *Great. That hurts.* He felt for the curb behind him and sat back on it rubbing his bruised elbow and flexing his leg to make sure other bones weren't broken. He was usually so sure-footed. Not here.

He closed his eyes again and lay back on the pavement, oblivious to the filth that probably coated it. He had to do something, but what? The incessant static grated on his nerves. He remembered what Gem had said about the despair that takes over a person in a place like this. *Fight it, Tom. Fight it.*

He thought of Willet again. It helped to think of her, so he held her image on the screen of his inner vision. She smiled at him and puckered her lips in a kiss. He could almost feel the softness of her lips on his. She began to sing. He couldn't hear her at first, but then he could. She was chanting the word Gem had taught them. Her voice chimed. He repeated the words with her over and over until his breath slowed and his jangled thoughts calmed. Whatever would be would be. *Wasn't there a song like that?* The knot in his stomach eased. It felt good to let it go. He lay there for a while, drifting and dreaming, not feeling the need to do anything. There were stories in the news about people lost in some wilderness with no ability to navigate, how they got more and more lost until they gave up and died. He could relate. He might die here. It seemed like an actual possibility the more he thought about it.

A warm hand suddenly touched his knee. Startled, he gulped and sat up.

The Traveler

The Traveler explained long ago to the Circle that she traveled by folding spacetime, touching one point in space and time to another to form a kind of corridor. Then travel was a matter of walking into one doorway and out another. How she managed this was impossible to figure out from watching her. She stood with eyes closed and hummed HU, spoke other words in Spanish. The air hummed with her, and then a door in spacetime folded open into a different space and time. Or time sped by, and they ended up in the same place but at a different time. In any case, the trip was usually instantaneous and a bit dizzying. This particular trip didn't feel like the others they had taken with the Traveler. There was movement, and it was more jolt than flow. Momentum swung forward and back and forward again until everyone felt queasy. Suddenly, they were suspended in midair, their feet dangling.

"A bit of flux and uncertainty," Sonrisa said. "A void could be forming here."

"The floating is nice," Willet said. "And it's quiet. The voices are gone."

Rock and Roll Dreams

Dean followed the siren song of screaming guitars and pounding drums down the dark stairway to the club floor. The bass beat pulsed in his feet and pounded against his chest. He had to get closer, close enough to feel it in every muscle. He entered the main room where a four-piece rock band played on a stage. The music coursed through his blood with an inexplicable feeling of power that set his teeth on edge. The beat lifted him to that level of exaltation that had made him want to be a rock musician since he first heard Led Zeppelin on his father's CDs.

A singer fronted the band with harmonica in hand and a cascade of curly black hair flopping around his face. He howled and grimaced in song, and then wailed on the harmonica. Dean didn't care if the lyrics were good or if there was a melody. Everything he felt about the ecstatic energy of rock and roll was conveyed in the pounding beats and the urgent squeal of that harmonica. It was so raw, so beautiful. He felt ready to jump out of his skin. If he couldn't pound on some drums soon, he'd have to punch his fists into a wall. The big set of black and silver chrome Ludwig drums and the Zildjian cymbals on stage called to him. He itched to be up there, in the flow of the music. And then a woman's voice whispered in his head. "Go ahead. Play the drums. Sing. You know you want to. Stay with me, and you will always have a band and a stage." *Yeah, I could stay here forever, just play music. Why not? I don't want to go back.*

Circus of Cruelty

TJ climbed the lattice of beams and two-by-fours above the laser room with muscles screaming. At the top, he caught his heaving breath and examined the ceiling. A square section cut into it looked like the entrance to an attic. He pushed on the loose square of wood and lifted it, slid it out of the way and peeked his head up through the opening into another room. The room smelled of paint. The walls were blank white. A long bank of windows on one side let in dreary light that reflected off the top of a metal office desk in the middle of the room. TJ pulled himself up through the opening in the floor and limped to the desk. He shuffled through the drawers, found nothing in them. Then he noticed two mounds of ice, a large one next to the desk and a much larger one against the far wall. *I must have a head injury. Why would there be ice in here?*

He heard a bell ring and turned to the elevator. The doors opened. *It's working!* Despite his sore and weary body, he stumbled toward it, got in and hit the button for the thirty-sixth floor where he had last seen Jonah. TJ prayed nothing bad had happened to the boy. At floor thirty-six, the doors slid open on the circus scene he remembered. He stepped out. A juggler walked by, tossing flaming knives in the air. TJ turned out of his way, bumping into the clown with the red fright wig and saggy brown suit who hissed at him through clenched teeth. TJ ignored him. "Jonah", he called out as loud as he could. "Jonah, where are you?"

A cacophony of laughter, growls, caws and roars answered his call. He walked up and down the rows past rings, trapezes and tents. It appeared to be a regular circus, but it made him feel uneasy as he looked closer. Two clowns dressed as boxers punched each other in the face. Chimpanzees and tigers screamed at him, reaching through the bars of their cages with wicked-sharp claws. A ring master poked at an acrobat on a high swing with an electrified pole. The man cried out in pain and fell from his swing. He hit the ground with an ominous crunch of bones. The ring master laughed. This was a circus of cruelty, the only way to describe it.

TJ walked faster, avoiding vendors trying to shove black cotton candy in his face, and shouted for Jonah. Another clown wearing an old-fashioned police uniform with silver buttons tried to put a rope around his neck. TJ pushed him away and started sprinting through the circus, up one row of horrors and down another. He finally found the boy standing in front of a low stage. A naked woman, brown haired and young with her ankle chained to the stage, was being bitten repeatedly by a snake. She yelped and made futile attempts to protect herself with arms and hands. Jonah seemed mesmerized. He was so painfully young. A child should not see this. TJ grabbed Jonah's shoulders and turned him away from the bizarre scene. The boy's eyes were bleary and his jaw slack. *Is he drugged?*

"Jonah, look, it's me," he said, shaking him slightly and patting his cheeks. "Talk to me, please."

Jonah's eyes came into focus. "Mr. Tom, look," he said pointing at the woman. "The snake is biting her. That's so whack."

"This is a bad place, Jonah. We have to get out of here and find your mother." He took the boy's hand and led him back to the elevator that was still waiting with doors open. They got in, and TJ pressed fifth floor where Evelyn was last seen. The doors closed, and the elevator began to move, up instead of down. TJ pounded on the down button, but the elevator kept rising. At the eighty-ninth floor, the doors opened on the desk and the mounds of ice. The elevator didn't respond to the buttons TJ pushed, so he walked out and pulled Jonah behind him.

"We'll have to find another way down," he said. "There's a trap door in the floor. Just stick close to me."

He searched for the hole in the floor he had climbed through but couldn't find it. The opening had sealed and disappeared. He heard a muffled voice coming out of the mound of ice by the desk. It said, "Get me outta here."

Love and the Listener

Take it easy, Tommy boy. You almost sideswiped that truck. Stop thinking about her for a minute, will ya?

TJ had gone home for a couple of days to get his head back together after the inexplicable episode with Gem. Now he sped back to Hemmings to pick Willet up on Wednesday afternoon. He drove the S-class Mercedes that he leased for business, hoping it would be quiet enough for her not to wear the headphones. He didn't want her to get a headache.

They were going to his cabin in Big Bear for a couple of days of mountain scenery and fresh air. Willet looked pale and tired after the Circle experience. She needed to relax, forget all the craziness. He did too.

Since restaurants were too noisy, he planned a gourmet meal at the cabin. He enlisted the aid of his favorite LA chef, in whose restaurant, Le Rossignol, he had invested capital. Chef Andre was bustling around the kitchen at the cabin at that moment, preparing his signature coq au vin, pine nut raviolis, and braised spring vegetables. There would be something flambé for dessert. TJ had selected the wines himself, white, as the lady preferred. He also had a selection of Chopin in the car as well as at his cabin. She loved Chopin.

He looked at himself in the rearview mirror. *You haven't been this way about a woman since Valerie. Remember how that turned out.*

It was unfair to put Valerie Stanfield in the same category as Willet. Valerie, a garden variety spoiled brat, toyed with his heart in high school. Willet, on the other hand, could be a creature from another planet. She had seemed so fragile when he met her, ethereally beautiful, and kind of irritating. She turned out to be really smart, and so sweet. When they walked the beach together and talked, she started getting under his skin. It seemed very promising before all the insanity began. He barely recognized his own life anymore.

He shook himself out of reverie when he reached the road to Pine Siskin House and drove directly to the front door. The Mercedes barely purred, but Willet would still hear him coming. As soon as he pulled up, she opened the front door and stepped out on the porch. *Man, she sure looks fine.*

Willet had a long, cream-colored cashmere coat wrapped around her, and carried a small overnight bag. She carried a pair of headphones on her left arm. TJ got out and walked to the passenger side to open the door for her. When he took her bag and helped her into the car, he caught a waft of lavender and sage.

In the car, she let the coat drop off to reveal bare shoulders in a red silk tank top. Her long corn-silk hair draped over her shoulders and her eyes reflected the blue of the sky. He had to take a deep breath. She looked so beautiful.

"Hey, babe, you look hot," he nodded as he slid behind the wheel. His eyes slowly traced her slender neck and the swell of chest under red silk.

She blushed and smiled. "Thanks. I don't get to dress up much. And you look very GQ in your charcoal three-piece suit. I like the green stripe in the tie. It matches your eyes."

"This is my barrister suit. I had a meeting at court this morning."

"Nothing serious, I hope…"

"No, just fire 'victims' trying to sue me into bankruptcy."

"That sounds serious."

"Fortunately, there were no major injuries," he said as he put the car in gear and took off around the circular drive. "Smoke inhalation, some scrapes and burns. Fire investigators couldn't figure out what started the fire, and they didn't find any evidence of negligence on the part of the club, so that helps my case."

"It wasn't your fault! The rocks started the fire. They almost set Audrey's car on fire."

TJ gave a wry smile. "I can't tell a judge that evil rocks started the fire. I'd probably lose my license to practice law." He merged onto the freeway and stepped on the gas. The windows didn't whistle, and nothing rattled.

"This car is pretty quiet!" she said appreciatively. "So, we're going to your cabin for dinner? Are you cooking for me?"

"I thought about cooking, but I made other arrangements. Hope you like French."

"Mmm, French is my favorite."

"Excellent." He pressed Play on the CD, and the first of the Chopin Ballades began to play.

Willet looked at him with pleased surprise. She leaned over and pressed her lips to his cheek. TJ smiled to himself. *Good call on the music, Barlow.*

TJ navigated the streets of Big Bear to the gravel road leading to his cabin. He got out, opened Willet's door, and held out an arm to help her from the car. One slim leg stretched to the ground followed by the other. She took his arm. He nodded and grinned at her red croc stilettos.

"Thanks for the approval, Thomas Jefferson," she said. "You can stop ogling now."

"I'll be ogling all evening. It's on the menu."

She smiled and her cheeks flushed rose. She wrapped the coat around her and walked with him to the house. He unlocked the front door, waving her in with a flourish.

"Something smells delicious," she said as she sniffed the air and looked around. "Wow, this is a great place."

A table set for two filled a small dining area next to the kitchen. White linen, crystal glasses and silver glittered under lit candles. A bouquet of wildflowers graced the center of the table.

"Did you do all this?" she asked in wonder.

"I made menu selections. Chef Andre made it happen," he said as he shrugged his suit coat onto a chair and went into the kitchen. The chef's assistant had left wrapped dishes in the oven, staying warm. He poured two glasses of wine and returned to her.

"Sancerre," he said, handing her a glass. "It's a good vintage, hope you like it."

She studied the wine, turning the stem of the glass between her fingers. "The Loire Valley is my favorite part of France that I've never been to. That's where the castles are."

He grinned at her.

She blushed and murmured, "I'm not a wine snob, really."

"Glad to hear it. Otherwise, we'd have to do a blind taste test to see how good you really are. Do you want to unpack, freshen up?"

"No, I'd like to take a look at that wonderful view you have. Can I see the lake from here?"

He slipped his arm around her shoulders and led her out to the back deck. The rocky hills fell away from the deck, undulating in grey gorges that tumbled toward the lake. Stands of pines and aspen brushed the blue sky as far as the eye could see. Far below, sunlight flickered on the surface of Big Bear Lake. Snow-covered peaks rose around the lake. The air tasted as fresh and cool as it smelled.

They gazed at the view without speaking, and then he turned her in his arms and kissed her, soft and unhurried. He felt her shiver. "Are you cold? Want to go inside?"

"No, this is so lovely."

Her eyelids closed. She made a sound of quiet contentment. He leaned in to inhale the warm scent of her neck, pressed his lips to her ear and whispered. "You smell delicious, Red Riding Hood. I might have to take a bite."

Willet's eyes fluttered open to look at him.

He took her glass from her, placed it with his on a nearby table, and casually backed her against a wooden pillar of the porch. He wrapped a hand around her neck and pressed a deep kiss to her lips. She slipped her arms around his waist. He continued the kiss and slid his hands under her coat to grasp her torso. His thumbs brushed the sides of her breasts through the thin red silk. She drew a sharp breath and tried to move closer to him. He pulled back a little to look into her eyes.

"Are you hungry?" he murmured.

"You mean, for food?"

"We haven't even had the appetizers yet. Let's see what Chef Andre made for us." He took her hand, pulled her back into the cabin. She smiled a small smile and followed him to the dinner table. Beeswax candles filled the air with a light scent of honey. She slipped out of her coat and dropped it on a chair in front of the stone fireplace in the living room. A red silk skirt matching her silk tank top swirled around her legs as she turned to the table.

They ate chilled prawns with glasses of Sancerre. With the coq au vin, they drank an aged Sauvignon Blanc from Pessac Leognan, mellow with flavors of nuts and honey custard. Willet picked up a roll, broke it open and spread butter on one half with the butter knife. She savored the roll with closed eyes and a contented smile. Then she picked up the other half, slid the butter knife over it, and looked at TJ thoughtfully.

"I'm feeling as buttered as this roll," she said, matter-of-fact.

TJ cupped the glass in his palm, sipped the wine, and watched her over the rim. "Whatever do you mean?"

"Well, this is wonderful, of course. How many of your guests get the Chef Andre treatment?"

"It's not a 'treatment.' I've never done this for anyone else. I wanted you to relax and enjoy, that's all."

"I *am* enjoying myself, Thomas. After everything that's happened, it means a lot to me, being in this beautiful place with you. But now I know there are other stories going on behind what I see with my eyes. I'm questioning everything. Help me not to do that."

TJ sat back from the table and folded his arms. "Are you asking about other women coming here?"

"I guess I am, sort of, among other things…"

"There have seldom been women here, honestly. But now it will just be you."

Willet looked down at the table. "Are there sound prints in this room? Do I have to be careful?"

TJ chuckled. "You want to listen in, don't you? It's driving you crazy."

She looked up again. "No, I don't! The last time I listened in on your life, I didn't enjoy it."

"I've got nothing to hide. Go ahead and eavesdrop."

Willet took another bite of her roll, chewed slowly and looked at him, considering. "I think not," she said finally. "What I heard at your house really confused me, and I realized later I had no right. We haven't known each other that long. You've clearly had more of a life than I've had. That's not your fault."

There it is again, he thought, *good sense and self-assurance. I love that about her.* He put his glass down and leaned forward, making sure they were eye to eye.

"Despite what you may think, there haven't been that many women in my life. They've been around it, but not in it. I can count the actual relationships I've had on three fingers. I don't usually get serious." He paused, considering his words. "You've changed things, Will." As he said it, he realized how much.

"How have I changed things?" Her voice quivered.

"I trust you. That's rare for me. Besides, you're amazing."

She met his gaze. Thoughts and emotions flickered across her face.

"What's going on in that beautiful head of yours?"

"We haven't talked about the Circle, Thomas. What we saw and heard changes things too, changes life. Doesn't it, for you?"

He sat back with a sigh. "Ah yes, the Circle. I figured we'd get to that. Does it change life? I don't know. I've always felt like I had a pretty good grip on life, mine at least, and I tend to distrust things that don't make sense. What I saw that day made no sense, despite Gem's explanations. I didn't understand why I was chosen to see it."

"My friendship with Gem is important in my life. I'm a part of what she's doing now. The Circle is important to me." She paused, and her voice dropped almost to a whisper. "Is that a problem for us? Do you think I'm crazy? When we first met, you thought I was crazy."

"You look at things differently, that's for sure," he said. "You hear things the rest of us don't hear. I don't think you're crazy, no. You're – unique."

"What are you going to do about the Circle? Gem asked for our help. Will you help her?"

TJ paused before he spoke. "I've decided to suspend judgment for now. If I end up in that Circle again, flying through space, I won't be able to ignore it twice. I'll have to take it more seriously."

Willet smiled radiantly, got up and walked behind his chair, twined her arms around his neck and kissed him. "That works for now."

"Then we're agreed," he said solemnly. He pulled her into his lap. He raised her hands to his lips and kissed each one. "I'm in your hands."

The Ring Thrower

While Dean and Bart went off to confront the Wall of Unknowing like medieval knights challenging a dragon, Audrey du Place paced at the edge of Bart's crystal fields, fuming. She was left behind, the fragile damsel in a tower, and she didn't like it. All the visitors had departed, and the office closed. The eerie quiet unsettled her. At her feet, mounded rows of crystal pulsed with energy. Light reflected from a billion facets and prismed into rainbow colors. There was a faint ringing sound she hadn't noticed before. She felt both attracted and repelled by the crystal, wanting to touch the sparkling stuff but afraid to do so. The purity of the light proved too enticing to resist. She stepped into the field, crouched down and laid her palms over the mounds to feel the energy.

A warm current streamed up her arms. Her head swam. She pulled her palms away and stood swaying on her feet. Then she yanked off her shoes and pressed each bare foot against the crystal. The soles of her feet tingled. Energy surged up her legs, causing every nerve and muscle fiber to vibrate. It felt like liquid sunshine flowing in her blood. The rush of energy to her brain was so overwhelming, she had to hop out of the field onto the dirt path and catch her breath, but separation from the energy flow left her feeling deflated and sad. She brushed one hand lightly across a mound of crystal and then the other to regain that wonderful feeling. When she pressed both palms down, it was too much. Dizzy, she stumbled backward.

Her inner vision flooded with pictures, and her ears buzzed. Vivid memories assembled from fragmented images, of Bart guiding her through a smoke-filled room to an open doorway, of Dean pulling her away from a pile of rock and crystal that was about to tip over on top of her. She remembered a heated kiss from soft lips pressed urgently to hers and strong arms pulling her against a hard chest. She ached for that kiss, wanted to bury her fingers in dark brown hair and surrender to those muscles, but *which man was it*? An image of Dean flashed in her mind's eye. He kissed her before they jumped out of that flying pod to escape from the Underworld and said if they got another chance, they would take the time together they missed. He said he wanted more. She had wanted more too, so very much, but now? What did she really want?

And then another memory – of Bart leaning in to kiss her after the dinner she cooked for him. He had seemed like a good-hearted geek, but he wasn't shy. His kiss exuded a sexual heat that surprised her. At the time, she thought she'd like to explore those hidden depths, see where they led. Had time had run out? Two handsome heroes had saved her life. They both said they wanted her intimately. In simpler times, she might have been ecstatic over the possibilities, but so much had changed. She had changed. She craved something deeper now.

A staccato of loud crackles made her head spin to the right. It sounded like gunshot. Geysers of white light spewed out of the blurry darkness on the eastern horizon. Dean and Bart were there, confronting the Wall. A moment of panic split her conscious viewpoint in two, and she stepped away from her physical body into astral consciousness. Things looked different from that perspective. The crystal field looked like an island of dazzling light surrounded by darkness. Churning gray clouds crashed against the borders of the island, unable to break through. In the distance, the Wall turned deep purple and seething. It spit fire, shot spikes of lightning that hit the ground. If Dean and Bart didn't see what she saw, they had no idea how much danger they were in.

Her fingers got hot, and she looked at her hands. Small gold rings were spinning on every one of her fingers. Confusing, but familiar. She knew what to do. When she tapped her palms together to ease the stinging heat, the small rings melted into one larger ring, a foot in diameter. She spun the large ring on her right index finger. Instinct and memory took over. *I throw this ring before my hand burns, and I'll need a clear shot at that monstrosity out there.*

With that thought, her astral viewpoint expanded in great clarity. She hurled the ring toward the Wall like a Frisbee with all the force she could put behind it. It flew to the horizon and disappeared into the Wall's billowing darkness. Another set of rings appeared on her fingers. She merged them into an even bigger ring and sent it sailing. The Wall swallowed it and burped out a puff of gray smoke. Soon she was throwing rings from both hands as quick as they formed on her fingers. The Wall hurled barbs of lightning at her in response, but they fell short, unable to pierce the island of light on which she stood. She threw bigger and bigger rings until no more would form. Her astral consciousness closed, and she dropped back into her physical body. *Just need to lie down a minute and close my eyes. That's all.* Knees buckling, she slumped over and passed out.

The Spider's Lair

The Traveler took Audrey to the eighty-seventh floor of the

Dragon Head Building where she stepped out of a space-time

fold into a dark stairwell. A metal stairway was anchored to

the wall rose to a door on the next higher level. Audrey

walked to the stairs. "What are we doing here?" she asked.

"Be careful of the eighty-nineth floor," Sonrisa told her. "I

advise against stepping out directly on that floor. You can

begin here, and then climb the next two flights by stair. Enter

the top floor very quietly."

That sounded like good advice. "Are you coming too?"

Audrey asked.

"I am needed elsewhere for a past life reckoning," Sonrisa replied. "You are needed here. Proceed on your own for the moment. The Guardian will join you soon. Meanwhile, keep your wits about you and maintain your focus. This building is full of traps."

With those words of wisdom, Sonrisa closed her spacetime
fold and disappeared, leaving Audrey alone in the stairwell.
Cold dread washed over her at the thought of what she might
find up the stairs. She shivered and her insides quaked.
Having Gem or Sonrisa with her always gave her confidence.
She rode in the wake of their power and purpose when she
was with them, but she didn't feel so confident now that they
weren't at her back. She climbed the last flight of stairs with
footsteps as quiet as she could step, whispering the HU chant
under her breath to calm her pounding heart. She paused to
listen, wishing she had her sister's incredible hearing, but the
silence revealed nothing. At the top of the stairs, there was a
large black metal door. She reached for the chrome handle and
eased the door open, hoping it wouldn't squeak. A dark
hallway led to a second door with a crack of light showing at
the floor. She opened that door as quietly as she could and
entered a large room with rafters and high windows that were
streaked and dirty. The room felt warm and clammy, and fine

white dust floated in the air. A maze of white threads crisscrossed the room from wall to wall. Spider webs. This claustrophobic space had to be the spider's lair. A putrid smell of something decomposing made her stomach twist. She shuddered at the thought of what might cause that awful smell.

A familiar voice spoke softly near her ear. "Auddie, stay quiet, the spider is sleeping," her sister said. "Look up."

Audrey looked up. There was Black Widow Barbie, suspended by a single thread from a beam high in the ceiling. The spider hung upside down, long legs folded up onto her body. Spiders have to sleep often to restore their energy. A factoid from sixth grade science class. While the spider slept, Audrey might have time to do what she came to do – rescue Dean and get him out before the spider stirred. Like Willet said, 'Stay quiet."

www.ingramcontent.com/pod-product-compliance
Lightning Source LLC
Chambersburg PA
CBHW071128130626
46555CB00015B/2688